MOUNT ETNA
LAVA LEAP

BY S
ILLUSTRA

Book design by Jake Slavik
Illustrations by Carl Pearce

Photographs ©: Shutterstock Images, 67; Joe Scarnici/Getty Images Entertainment/Getty Images, 69

Published in the United States by Jolly Fish Press, an imprint of North Star Editions, Inc.

First Edition
First Printing, 2021

This is a work of fiction. Names, characters, places, and incidents are either the product of the author's imagination or are used fictitiously, and any resemblance to actual persons living or dead, business establishments, events, or locales is entirely coincidental.

Library of Congress Cataloging-in-Publication Data (pending)
978-1-63163-547-2 (paperback)
978-1-63163-546-5 (hardcover)

Jolly Fish Press
North Star Editions, Inc.
2297 Waters Drive
Mendota Heights, MN 55120
www.jollyfishpress.com

Printed in the United States of America

TABLE OF CONTENTS

CHAPTER 1

Jett Ryder gazed at the massive mountain in the distance. "Even from far away," he said, "it makes you feel small."

He was in a park south of Seattle with his best friend, Mika Moore. They both lived close by. It was a clear day, and Mount Rainier dominated the horizon, even though it was nearly a hundred miles to the south.

"It's a giant," said Mika. "Luckily, it's sleeping."

"Sleeping?" asked Jett.

"Mount Rainier is a volcano. But it hasn't erupted

since 1894." Mika was a history buff. She had more random facts about the past than any other twelve-year-old he knew. She probably even knew more than some adults. "Imagine if the volcano suddenly woke up," she said. "There could be smoke and ash and flaming lava shooting from the top."

"That would be awesome," said Jett. "Dangerous, but awesome."

Mika smiled. "Kinda like your stunts."

Jett returned her grin. He was the biggest name in motocross stunt riding. And, at twelve years old, he was also the youngest.

"It would be so cool to do a jump out there," he

said. The image of him soaring over Rainier's slopes flashed in his head.

Mika pushed up her glasses. "For you to clear Mount Rainier, we'd need to install a rocket booster on your bike. Probably two of them. And make the world's biggest crash pit. Along with a bike-sized parachute. Even then, the physics would be practically impossible."

Jett smiled. Not in a mocking way, but out of pure respect. Not only could Mika win any history trivia contest, but she was also an engineering genius. She and her team designed all of his stunts.

Jett knew he couldn't jump his bike over something

as big as Mount Rainier, but he still liked the idea of performing a stunt at a volcano. "What about a crater leap?"

A thundering clap of hands startled them both. Jett's dad had arrived. He was a mountain of a man himself, and his clap sounded like two boulders colliding. He was also Jett's co-manager. "A crater leap," he repeated. "Tell me more!"

Jett's dad looked back and forth between the two of them like a kid waiting for free candy.

"We were thinking about a trick at Rainier," said Jett.

His dad nodded, turning solemnly toward the

distant mountain. "Nothing competes with nature."

He paused a second for effect. Then he pointed to

the sky dramatically. "Except for a Jett Ryder jump!"

"Dad," said Jett.

"Well, this looks like a stunt discussion if I ever

saw one." Jett's mom had just walked up. She was

Jett's other co-manager.

"Jett's going to leap one of the craters at Mount

Rainier!" his dad told her.

"Is that even possible?" she asked.

Jett's parents often butted heads over his stunts.

His dad wanted big and bold. His mom did, too, but

she was more sensible about safety.

"It's not," answered Mika. "Mount Rainier's craters are both about a quarter-mile wide."

"Oh," said Jett. They all knew that was way out of jumping range.

"There must be something," said his dad. "Imagine the promotion we could do: Jett Ryder and the *Volcano Vault*!"

Mika thought a moment. "A lava stream might be narrow enough to jump over."

"Jett Ryder and the *Lava Launch*!" said Jett's dad in his over-the-top announcer's voice.

"Is there lava on Mount Rainier?" Jett's mom asked.

Mika shook her head. "Not unless it suddenly starts erupting. But other volcanoes have active flows, like Krakatoa and Tambora."

"Where are those?" asked Jett.

"Indonesia."

Jett thrilled at the idea of performing a stunt halfway across the world. "Could we do a jump that far away?"

"Here's the very person who would know," said his mom.

Mika's mother had just joined them. She was an attorney and handled all the paperwork for Jett's stunts. "Just tell me where," she said. "It may take a bit longer than usual to get permission, but I'll do my best to make it happen."

Jett and Mika looked at each other.

"We've never done a stunt on another continent," Jett said.

"It would be like going to a new school," Mika added. "We'd have to prove ourselves all over again."

Jett thought that sounded both scary and exciting. Which was right up his alley. "I'm always game for a new challenge. You?"

Mika smiled, then held up a hand. "Hello, rest of the world. Get set . . ."

Jett gave her a fist bump in return. ". . . for Jett!"

CHAPTER 2

Jett's dad was beside himself with excitement. "An international stunt! We'll *Crack Open Krakatoa*!"

Jett sometimes thought his dad got as much excitement coming up with new stunt names as he did watching the actual stunts themselves. Jett, Mika, and their parents were all back at Jett's house, planning the volcano leap.

"What was the other volcano you mentioned?" Jett asked Mika.

Her eyes lit up. "Tambora. It's the site of the most powerful eruption ever recorded."

"Ohhh," said Jett's dad. "I like the sound of that."

Mika paced the room. "It was 1815. When Tambora blew, it erupted for four whole months. The skies were so cloudy with ash that even a year later, thousands of miles away in Europe, people experienced what they called the *Year Without a Summer.*"

Jett looked out a window and tried to imagine the sun blotted out. For the whole summer.

"A group of writers got together at a house in Switzerland," Mika continued. "Surrounded by all that gloomy darkness, they challenged each other to make up scary stories. That's where *Frankenstein* came from. And one of the first vampire tales."

"Whoa," said Jett. "It's like the volcano created those monsters!"

"If we did a stunt there," said his dad, "we could call it the *Creature Crater*!"

Mika opened her laptop and did some research. But after a few minutes, she frowned. "Both Krakatoa and Tambora have lava flows, but I don't think we'll be able to jump them."

"Why not?" asked Jett.

"Both mountains are surrounded by thick jungles and are probably too remote to access. And their lava streams are on areas that are really, really steep. We need someplace flatter to do a jump."

"What about Mount Etna?" offered Mika's mom.

"Etna!" said Jett's dad. "That's in Italy, right?"

"It is," said Mika. "On the island of Sicily." She pulled up some images on her computer. "Mount Etna is the tallest active volcano in all of Europe."

"Perfect!" said Jett's dad.

"Tall isn't good, honey," said Jett's mom. "That means steep."

"Ah, right."

"But," Mika said, "Etna does have active lava channels that are pretty far down from the summit on fairly flat terrain."

"Perfect!" said Jett's dad again, grinning.

Mika pulled up some maps on the computer, along with satellite images. "It looks like some of Etna's lava channels are less than one hundred feet wide."

"I can definitely make it across one of those," said Jett.

"But you'll need to stay a good distance from the lava the whole time," said his mom. "It'll be too hot to get anywhere close."

"That's true," agreed Mika. "We'll probably need a safety buffer of another hundred feet on each side. Which means the total jump would be more like three hundred feet."

Jett let out a low whistle. "That's far, but still doable." He thought of Tambora, erupting so intensely it changed history. "Volcanoes are some of the most powerful things on Earth. It would be amazing to do a stunt there, at Mount Etna. We could call it the *Mount Etna Lava Leap*!"

His dad nodded. "That will draw a crowd for sure. But can we make the stunt more exciting? Right now, it's just jumping a stream of lava."

"*Just*?" said Jett's mom.

Jett thought a moment. "What if we sprayed water on the lava? That would make steam. Which would look like I'm jumping through an eruption."

"Now you're talking!" said his dad.

"Excuse me," said his mom, "but won't steam from lava be boiling? Or hotter?"

"I'm on it," said Mika. She tapped away at her computer. After a short time, she looked up. "It actually doesn't matter what the temperature is.

Because it's from lava, the steam will have sulfuric acid in it."

"Is that bad?" asked Jett's dad.

Mika pushed up her glasses. "It will eat right through Jett's stunt suit."

Jett's dad turned a little red. "Okay . . . that's pretty bad."

Instinctively, Jett scratched at his shirt sleeves.

"We could use regular fireworks," said Mika. "If we set them off beside the jump ramp, it would look like Jett is jumping through an eruption. Without the suit-eating part."

Jett's dad stood. "I like it!"

His mom sighed. "I'm still picturing my son being dissolved by a plume of acidic steam. But if it's just standard fireworks . . . those seem safe enough. But I'm not the one who'll be doing the stunt. Jett, what do you think?"

Jett knew every stunt was a balance between not being too dull and not being too dangerous. "My record is over three hundred feet. If we can find a lava stream narrow enough, I can do it. And I'll practice till perfect like always. If it's too risky when we check it out, I won't perform the stunt."

"And I won't let him," added Mika.

Jett knew his mom trusted Mika as much as he did.

"All right," his mom said. "Mount Etna it is."

Jett's dad leaned in. "After this, I bet they'll rename it Mount *Jett*-na!"

Everyone groaned.

CHAPTER 3

Jett sped across the bumpy dirt. He shifted gears almost without thinking, his trusty bike's two-stroke engine letting out a joyful *braaap!* as he increased speed.

Both families had arrived on the island a few days earlier. Mika's mom had secured the necessary paperwork and permissions, then rented a practice field outside of Etna Park. Now Jett was taking his first ride on Sicilian soil.

He aimed for a ramp-like mound of dirt, dropped his body weight down through the pegs, then pushed off as he rode up the dirt face. A second later, he was soaring.

Jett loved motocross riding. He loved the breathtaking speed of racing across the ground. He loved the thrumming power of his bike engine. But more than anything, he loved the jumps.

This wasn't a particularly high jump, but that didn't matter. As Jett flew through the air, the wind and breeze and even gravity itself seemed to laugh along with him. Back home, he had wondered if jumping would feel different here, halfway around the world.

It didn't. It was just as thrilling as always.

He landed perfectly, with both tires hitting at the same time. Then he rode in a slow, wide circle. Jumping here was the same, but one thing was very different: the view. No matter where he was, no matter where he looked, it seemed like Mount Etna was always there. If Mount Rainier had dominated the horizon, Mount Etna *was* the horizon.

And unlike Mount Rainier, Etna definitely wasn't asleep. It puffed a constant stream of smoke from its top as if it was breathing. It almost seemed like the mountain was half awake, watching. The tiniest tremor of fear shivered through Jett. Riding in Etna's shadow, he felt like a gnat next to a dragon.

Jett brought his bike to a crawl. He was sure the ground had trembled, just slightly. But maybe it was only his bike's engine vibrating. Or his heart pounding.

"You okay, Jett?" Mika's voice crackled in his headset.

He shook himself out of it. "Yup, just admiring the view. I can't believe it's smoking."

"That's not even the half of it," said Mika. "Beneath Mount Etna are millions of tons of red-hot magma. It might erupt at any moment. It could even spew all the way here, cover this whole practice field in liquid fire."

Jett wanted to tell her that she wasn't helping. "Cool . . ." he said.

"Ready for the practice jump?" asked Mika.

"Always," said Jett. He turned his focus away from the simmering mountain and to the long ramp that Mika's team had set up.

They couldn't practice on Mount Etna itself, because Mika's mom had only gotten permission for him to jump there on the day of the stunt. It would also take a while to build a smooth track over Etna's rough, rocky ground. Mika's team was up there now, getting it ready.

Before they had left, her crew had built a set of

ramps at the practice field. They were the same size as the ones on the mountain would be. Mika's team always tried to make practice conditions as close as possible to the real thing.

Jett sped toward the first ramp. This jump would be almost as long as his personal best. He went wide open on the throttle. The air whistled in his helmet, the shrubs and landscape rushing by. In the corner of his eye, Mount Etna loomed, unmoving. No matter how fast he went, it stayed put.

Jett reached the base of the ramp. He felt the familiar thrill, the anticipation of pure speed through air. He was in attack position, perfectly balanced on his bike. He lowered himself slightly, rode the long incline up, then pushed off the edge.

Jett was flying across the sky. Who needed rocket boosters? He felt at one with his bike, the air parting as he streaked higher.

Seconds later, Jett reached the crest. Somehow he always knew exactly when he was at the high point of a jump—exactly when he would start back toward the earth. It was the same way he always knew exactly how much speed and angle and arc he needed off the ramp. While Mika was great at figuring out the physics on paper, Jett somehow *felt* the physics in his whole body.

Gravity was easing him back toward the ground. He focused on the landing ramp ahead. This was such a long jump! It was the same distance he would need to clear on Mount Etna to make sure he was out of the lava channel's "hot zone."

Jett kept the bike steady while keeping himself balanced and even. Then, just before he reached the landing ramp, he tilted the front of the bike lower to match the ramp's downward angle. His wheels hit the ramp with a controlled slam, and the bike's suspension absorbed the impact of the landing perfectly.

Jett let out an excited whoop. He'd cleared the

jump distance with no problem. Doing the same thing

on the mountain would be a snap.

A second later, he nearly fell off his bike.

A crackling explosion rumbled across the sky.

High atop Mount Etna, a gush of bright lava shot up. It sprayed like a tiny fountain, then fell back down and disappeared.

Jett brought his bike to a slow stop. It wasn't an eruption, just a little burst of lava. Mika had told him those happened all the time. He knew that it wasn't something to be afraid of. Still, this was the first one he'd actually seen. He could feel the sheer power of it all the way from here. And if that was just the beginning of what Etna was capable of . . .

A trickle of sweat made its way down Jett's back. The mountain had seemed to belch its fire right *after* Jett thought how easy it would be to do the jump.

Almost like the mountain was laughing at him. Or giving him a warning.

CHAPTER 4

Jett spent the next several days on the practice field. He performed the jump over and over. Etna rumbled and spewed trails of smoke, but it didn't unleash another lava fountain.

"Practice till Perfect" was his number one motto, and this stunt was no different. Finally, he'd made the jump so many times he felt like he could do it with his eyes closed. He was ready to add the fireworks.

Jett kick-started his bike and rode to the far edge of the field. Today he was wearing a heavier, thicker practice suit than normal. Mika had added an outer layer for extra heat protection. She said he would need it for the lava, even from a hundred feet away.

Mika had also put a ventilator in Jett's helmet. That was in case the smoke from the fireworks blew too close. It was the same outfit he would wear for the actual stunt, just without his logo and sponsor decals.

The jump ramp was dead ahead. Jett focused on it, shifting gears seamlessly as he accelerated. Out of the corner of his eye, he saw Etna puffing its tiny cloud as usual. As his bike engine revved louder, he imagined Etna doing the same, turning its little cloud into a massive plume.

He pictured it erupting like Tambora, with its enormous explosion that had blocked a whole summer. That volcano had created monsters that were still alive in stories today.

Jett kicked the bike into high gear and kicked the thoughts from his head. Mount Etna wasn't erupting and darkening the sky. It was just calmly steaming at the top, like it always did. On its lower slopes, lava was inching along in flat, narrow rivers. And he was going to leap across one of them. Like this!

Jett accelerated toward the base of the ramp. A second later, the air crackled and popped with the fireworks that Mika's team had prepared. They shot from each side of him like streaks of red and orange fire.

Then the wind shifted. The smoke from the fireworks blew right into Jett's path. He could barely see the far edge of the ramp. Still, he kept going and rode it upward, the same as he had in the other practice jumps. Then he went soaring into the air.

But now the air was thick with smoke. This wasn't like the other practice jumps.

All around him, dense smoke swirled. The sky was dull gray, like the sun had been blotted out. He imagined the smoke had streaked down from Etna, full of monsters.

Instinctively, he reached up and waved it away.

The bike turned in response. Jett immediately

grabbed both handlebars again, trying to straighten

himself out.

He shot out of the smoke and into clear sky. Up ahead, he saw the landing ramp, just like always. He had plenty of height and distance, just like always. But he had veered to the side. Waving the smoke away had thrown him off course!

Mika spoke in his headset: "Jett, you're too far over. You have to do a dirt landing."

He fought back a wave of fear. "I know."

"You've got this, Jett."

He didn't have time to respond.

BAM!

The bike hit the ground, and Jett felt like he was going to push right through it—like he was going to sink straight under the earth. His suspension maxed out, and Jett popped back up. For a split second, he thought he would keep the bike upright. But the landing had jolted him so hard that he'd yanked the handlebars sideways.

Jett's engine roared, and he imagined it was Etna letting out a deep chuckle.

The bike spun out of control, and Jett flew off. He hit the ground, tumbling head over heels across the rocky dirt.

Jett wasn't sure where he was. His ears were ringing. Then he turned over and saw Etna looming

above him. A second later, his mom was at his side. She knelt and took his hand.

No matter where or when he wrecked, Jett's mom was always the first one there.

"Jett? Can you hear me?"

He nodded.

"Does anything feel broken?"

Jett flexed his arms and legs. They were sore but otherwise seemed okay. "I don't think so."

His mom breathed a sigh of relief. "It's a good thing you're wearing a thicker jump suit. I'm sure it helped absorb some of that crash."

Jett tried to push himself up, but his mom put

a hand, gently, on his chest. "Stay still for a few minutes."

She kept her hand there. It reminded Jett of his first bad racing wreck. He'd been leading the pack, but he'd taken a corner too fast and lost control. He'd crashed headfirst into a hay bale. Somehow, his mom had leaped over the track fence and rushed out to him. She'd put a hand on his chest, just like she was doing now. He'd instantly felt better. Then she'd walked him off the track.

The other racers had made fun of him that day for having his mom help him. The next day, Jett had gotten back on his bike and outraced everyone. He'd

won every single heat. None of them had laughed
after that.

His mom took her hand from his chest.

"Feeling better?" she asked.

"Yeah."

"What happened?"

He thought of how he'd imagined the sky full of
monsters.

"I lost focus," he said. "I let the smoke get to me."

"Smoke can really throw you. It happened to me
during a stunt, too."

"You did stunts?"

Jett knew his mom had been a world-class

motocross racer before he was born. In fact, she was the one who had taught him to ride. But she'd never mentioned doing stunts.

"I only did one," she said. "That was more than enough for me."

"What did you jump over?"

She smiled. "I didn't have your talent for jumps. I did a firewall."

Jett had seen those stunts at arena events. Event workers literally set a wall of wood on fire, and then you had to ride through it—by smashing the boards with your front tire and your helmet. He looked at his mom in total awe.

"There were two firewalls," she continued. "I broke through the first one okay. But then everything was smoke and heat. I was so scared that I had to shut my eyes."

Jett swallowed. He tried to put himself in his mom's shoes. "You rode blind?"

"I think that's what actually saved me. It was no use trying to see in that mess. But with my eyes shut, I could *feel* the ride. I felt my way through the second firewall." She shuddered. "I never want to do that again."

Jett nodded. "That's what it's like for me with jumps. I can feel them."

"I know. You're the most natural jumper I've ever seen. That's the only reason I let you do these crazy stunts."

Jett felt a rush of pride.

"Smoke is scary," his mom said. "We can lose the fireworks. It'll still be an amazing jump, even if it doesn't look like Mount Etna is erupting."

Jett realized that for the first time since they'd been here, he couldn't see the mountain. His mom, kneeling beside him, was blocking it out. It was still true that Etna was one of the most awesome things he had ever encountered. But it was no match for his mom.

"Let's keep the fireworks," he said. "I can do it."

CHAPTER 5

It was the day of the stunt. Other than the wisps of smoke coming from Mount Etna, the sky was crystal clear.

Jett wheeled his bike to the starting point. Mika's team had built a set of ramps on a flat area of the mountain, about halfway down from the summit. Jett hadn't thought it was possible, but Etna looked even more gigantic up close.

"How're you feeling?" Mika asked in his headset. She was set up on the other side of the jump.

"Pretty good."

"You're nervous. I can hear it in your voice."

Beyond the first ramp, past the one-hundred-foot safety zone, the lava river oozed, glowing orange-red. Even from this far away, Jett could feel its heat.

"Nah," he said. "I'm fine."

"This jump is exactly the same dimensions as on the practice field," Mika said.

"I know. Only, instead of dirt, I'll be leaping across flesh-eating fire."

As if on cue, a bubble of lava hissed and popped. Jett caught the faint stench of sulfur.

"We can call it off," Mika said. "Do something else. Go somewhere else."

Jett turned away from the lava. A large crowd was gathered around the starting point. They all held tiny flags—American ones, Italian ones, and others Jett didn't recognize. There was a similar crowd on the other side of the jump, at the end point. Jett thought of what Mika had said. Being in a new country was like going to a new school, and they had to prove themselves all over again.

"We're not calling off the jump," he answered. "Let's do this."

Jett kick-started his bike, and the crowd cheered, waving the tiny flags wildly.

"*Buongiorno*!" said Jett's dad, his voice booming

over the speakers. "Welcome, friends and fans across the globe! Welcome, one and all, to Jett Ryder and the *Mount Etna Lava Leap*!"

Drones whizzed by overhead, ready to capture Jett's every move on video. TV crews were set up at the start and end points of the jump. A huge audience would be watching the stunt live on screens all over the world.

Jett did his signature move: a double donut. First, he put one foot on the ground and rode his bike in a circle around it. Then he switched to the other foot and did the same thing, creating a figure eight. He had done the same move at his very first jump to calm his nerves. Now he did it at the start and finish of every stunt for good luck.

"Prepare yourself," Jett's dad announced, "for a feat never before seen! A breathtaking, fireworks-filled leap across a channel of molten lava, poured fresh from the earth's fiery depths!" He paused, then turned to Etna's summit. "We ask you, mightiest of mountains, for safe passage. And we ask all of you here to make the same request . . . with your applause!"

The crowd erupted with clapping, whistles, and cheers. Several people jumped in place. Jett swore he could feel the ground shake. For a split second, he wondered if Etna was rumbling. If so, he hoped it was cheering, just like the crowd.

Jett twisted the throttle and raced forward.

The track leading to the jump ramp was long and straight. The first part was crammed with spectators. Then the crowd thinned. Soon he was all alone, the sides of the track empty. It was too hot for anyone to stand here.

He caught a glimpse of the lava far ahead. It was a seeping, glowing river of orange. It looked like the sun had dripped fire onto the ground.

Jett shifted gears and went wide open on the throttle. He was hurtling at top speed now.

Suddenly, the air popped and cracked. But Jett didn't panic. He knew it was the fireworks. Streamers of yellow and orange shot up along the ramp.

Jett focused on the narrow space between them. But an instant later, it was filled with smoke. The wind had shifted, just like at practice.

"Jett?" Mika's voice sounded in his headset. "How's your visibility?"

He could barely see the front of the ramp.

"Good enough," he told Mika through clenched teeth.

A split second later, Jett was speeding up the ramp. Then he soared off and felt the familiar lift of riding the air. But he couldn't see a thing. There was nothing but thick, choking smoke.

Even with the ventilator Mika had installed, he could still taste the ash in the air. Fear shot through him. Maybe this smoke wasn't from the fireworks. Maybe that fountain of lava really had been a warning. To not come here. To not leap across Etna's rivers of fire.

"Safe passage," he whispered, echoing his dad's request. "Please."

Jett was flying completely blind now, hurtling alone on his bike through an ash-gray cloud that was hanging over a burning cauldron of lava. He wasn't even sure which way was up anymore. He wasn't going to make it!

Then he heard his mom's voice: "I could *feel* the ride. I think that's what saved me."

Jett closed his eyes.

The heat from the lava was more intense than

ever. It felt like it was eating through his boots. Jett fought back the panic. His boots. On his feet. Now he knew which way was down.

Jett focused everything he had on his bike. He felt himself soaring through the air, like he'd done hundreds of times before. He was at the crest now, the high point of the jump.

He opened his eyes.

For a moment, everything was still a gray haze. Then he burst through the smoke and into clear blue sky. He could see the landing ramp ahead!

But he still had a long way to go. And he was

dropping much faster than in practice. Had all that smoke slowed him down too much?

Jett sailed through the air, willing his bike to keep going.

Just another few feet . . .

At the last second, he tilted the front wheel down. And then *BAM!* He landed at the perfect angle, matching the downward slope of the ramp.

The bike wobbled from the impact, but Jett kept it steady. He rode down the ramp until he'd safely leveled out. Then he braked to a stop, and he looked around.

The crowd was going crazy!

"Jett!" Mika said in his headset. "You did it! And the smoke from the fireworks was amazing! When you came out, it looked like *you* were erupting from it! Like you were part of Etna!"

Jett did his signature double-donut move. Then he faced the summit.

The massive mountain could have erupted. It could have swallowed him whole.

But it hadn't.

Like his dad had said, you can't compete with nature. And Jett didn't want to. Instead, he felt like he was part of it—like maybe he really had erupted from Etna. Just a speck, just the tiniest fraction of

its raw, unpredictable power. Which was more than enough.

Jett sat taller in his seat. He felt both small and immense at the same time.

He had made it through. He had been given safe passage.

"Thank you," he said. And then he gave a tip of his helmet to the mightiest of mountains.

FOCUS ON
MOUNT ETNA

A LIVING GIANT

Mount Etna is located in Sicily, Italy. Towering approximately 10,900 feet (3,320 m) high, it is one of the largest volcanoes in Europe. It is also one of the most active. At times, Etna almost seems alive. It regularly belches steam and ash from its top. It also exhales chunks of rock, scattering them a few feet downhill. Locals call these rocks "lava bombs." Sometimes Etna shoots small bursts of lava. And it has lava flows, like the one Jett leaped, oozing from many different areas. The lava may not move fast, but it is hot. It can reach temperatures of more than 1,980 degrees Fahrenheit (1,080°C).

ERUPTIVE HISTORY

Etna has erupted many times over the centuries. Most times were harmless, but an eruption in 1983 destroyed

the tourist center near the top. One of the most destructive eruptions happened in 1669. Some of the hardened lava from that eruption can still be found in the nearby city of Catania. The citizens of Catania refer to Etna's 1669 eruption as "the Great Disaster."

CONSTANT CHANGE

Etna's size and shape change all the time. Some changes are small, like the falling lava bombs. Others are slow, like the creeping lava flows. And others, like an eruption, can make sweeping transformations in a hurry. Scientists are constantly monitoring the mountain to record its small shifts—and to predict the next big ones.

THAT'S AMAZING!

VICKI GOLDEN'S RIDE OF FIRE

What's it like to ride a motorcycle through a flaming wall of wood? The heat can reach 2,000 degrees Fahrenheit (1,090°C). The air is thick with smoke. And the only way to break through is to smash the blazing boards apart with your front tire—and your helmet.

Sound incredibly tough? Imagine doing it thirteen times in a row. That's exactly what motocross champion Vicki Golden did on July 7, 2019, to set the firewall world record. Golden did it for a live TV event honoring legendary daredevil Evel Knievel. Knievel had never been able to ride through that many walls of fire. But Golden pulled it off.

First, Golden put on a thick suit of fire-resistant material. Then, her team doused each wall with lighter fluid. The walls were spread out along an 850-foot-long (260-m-long) track at an airport in California. Her team set each wall ablaze, and then she rode her Indian FTR 1200 S motorcycle straight at them.

Golden smashed through the first wall at more than 30 miles per hour (48 km/h). As she went through, a chunk of burning board landed in her lap. Then the wind picked up, gusting at more than 20 miles per hour (32 km/h). The wind fanned the remaining firewall flames nearly 30 feet (9.1 m) high.

But Golden kept going and made it safely through every wall. Afterward, she said the stunt was so hard that she had lost track of how many firewalls there were.

GLOSSARY

attack position

The main motocross riding position for increasing speed and approaching jumps. The rider is standing, bending forward at the waist, knees slightly bent, elbows high, and looking forward.

crash pit

A large area at the base of a motocross stunt, usually walled-in and filled with large foam chunks or blocks. It helps break a rider's fall.

donut

A move where a rider puts one foot down and spins the bike around while riding in place, creating a circle on the ground.

kick-started

Started an engine by stepping down on the bike's lever.

motocross

Off-road dirt bike racing, usually done on dirt tracks with jumps.

pegs

Short metal bars that extend at foot level on either side of a motocross bike, which a rider can use for support.

suspension

A system on a bike's wheels that absorbs the shocks of bumps and landings.

throttle

A twistable grip on the dirt bike's right handlebar, which can be turned to increase or decrease engine power.

two-stroke engine

A type of engine that tends to use more fuel and is louder than a four-stroke engine, but is lighter and can work upside down.

wide open

When the throttle is turned to increase engine power to its maximum.

ABOUT THE AUTHOR

Sean Petrie writes books for kids, including *Welders on the Job* and *Crash Corner*. He also writes poetry, usually on the spot on a 1928 Remington typewriter. His poetry books include *Typewriter Rodeo* and the Seattle-based *Listen to the Trees*. He lives in Austin, Texas.

ABOUT THE ILLUSTRATOR

Carl Pearce lives in north Wales with his wife, Ceri. When not lost in his illustration work, he enjoys watching films, reading books, and taking long walks along the beach. He graduated from the North Wales School of Art and Design as an illustrator. His first book was published on his graduation day in 2004. He has since gone on to illustrate countless books for children.